Samy Mou
Who is the

By Emma Kamal

Copyright © 2023 Emma Kamal
All rights reserved. No part of this book may be reproduced without prior written permission of the publisher, except where noted in the text and in the case of brief quotations and reviews.

Illustration By
Mightokondria

Its Tuesday morning, what time is it now?
Can you read the clock?
It's school time,
Samy is still asleep can you help wake him up?

Let's call out his name softly,
and rub his little cheek,

"Samy, Samy , Samy."
Well done Samy is awake!

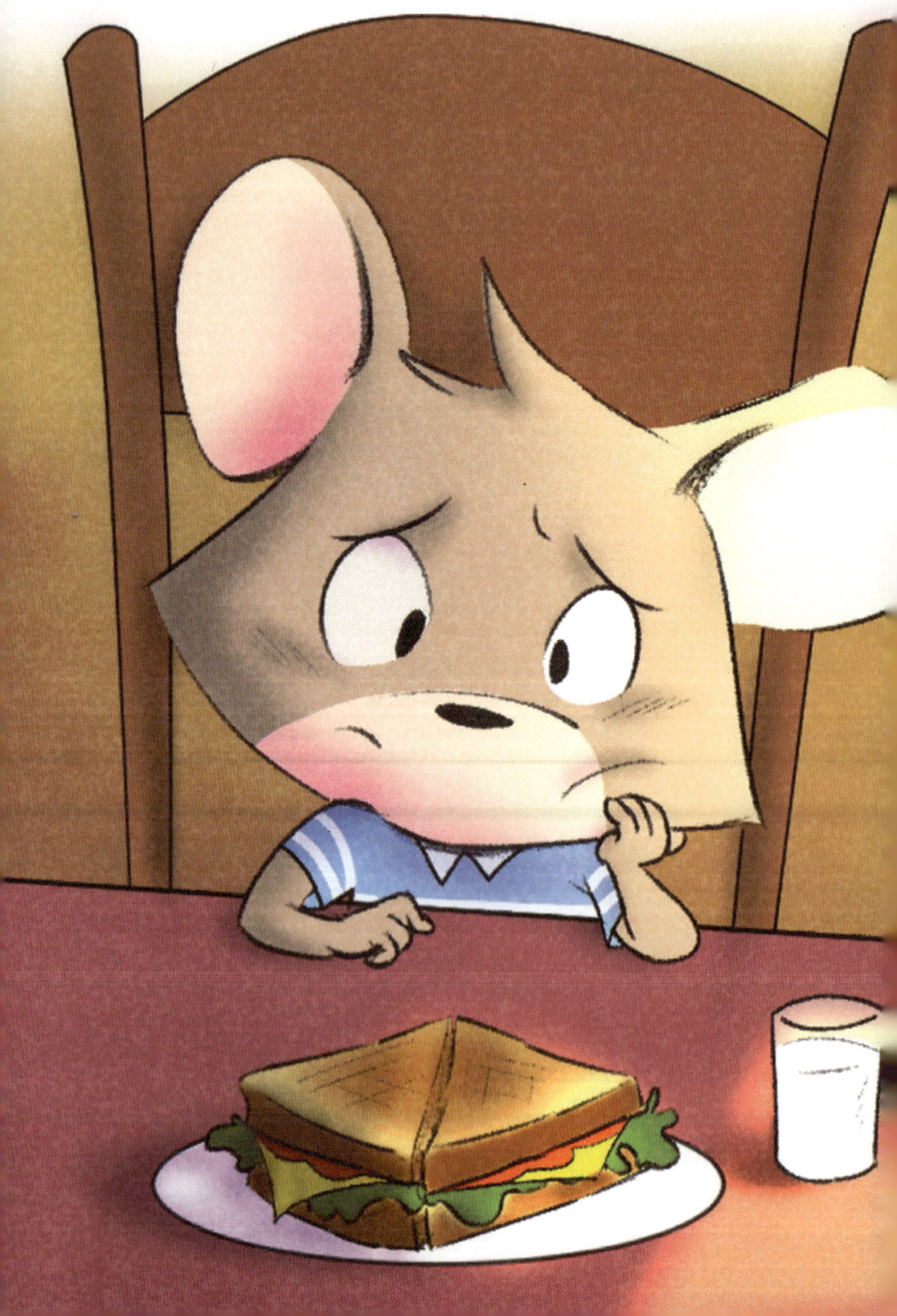

Samy is ready for school now, but wait,
He doesn't look cheerful today,
I wonder what's wrong?

Can you ask Samy whats wrong,
"Samy, what's wrong?
You don't look happy today?"

You can pat his arm, this will
make him feel better!

Samy looked at Mummy with sad eyes and said,

"I'm scared, I don't want to go to school, Pip takes my things and makes fun of me!" Poor Samy, can you calm him? you can say, "Don't cry Samy, and pat his head.

Mummy said lovingly, "That's fine Samy we all feel scared sometimes, but remember what we learnt from Brave Jack?"
Samy Nodded

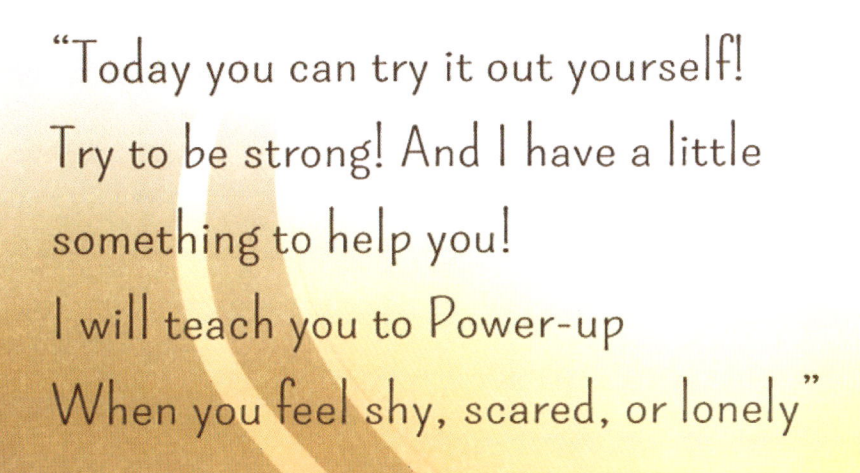

"Today you can try it out yourself!
Try to be strong! And I have a little something to help you!
I will teach you to Power-up
When you feel shy, scared, or lonely"

Wow, that looks interesting, can you help Samy Power up ?

"Stand Up!" Mummy said loudly, standing to how Samy how to power up.
"Tilt your head to one side,
all the naughty thoughts will slip out!"

Whuut

"Give it a tuck on the head to make sure it all went out,"

"Tuck, Tuck, Tuck!"

"That's great, now shake your body to let that unpleasant feeling in your tummy fall off!"

Shake, Shake, Shake!

"Swing your arms into the air to send them far away,"

Swooooooooosh!

"Now, Put your hands on your hips, turn around and say,"

"TADADA, TADADA TA DA DADA"

"There, here is my Superhero Samy"

POOF

Samy giggled, "That was funny Mummy," and sure enough like magic, the unpleasant feeling in his tummy was gone!

He gave Mummy a big warm hug, don't you want to try it as well?

Go on give Mummy a hug too, Wow, that was lovely!

At school, his tummy was playing tricks again so Samy did his power up before going into class. Can you remember the steps, can you help Samy?

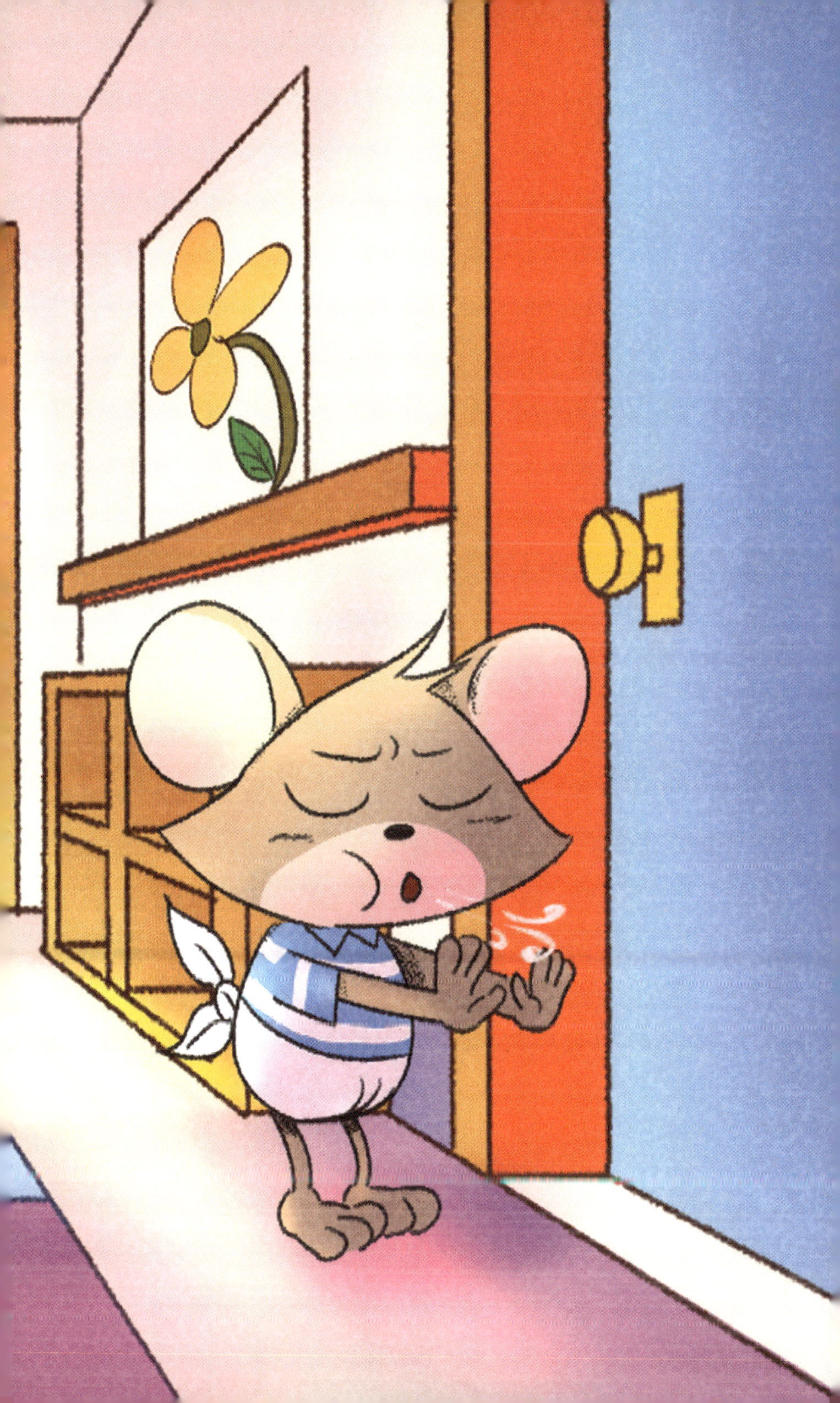

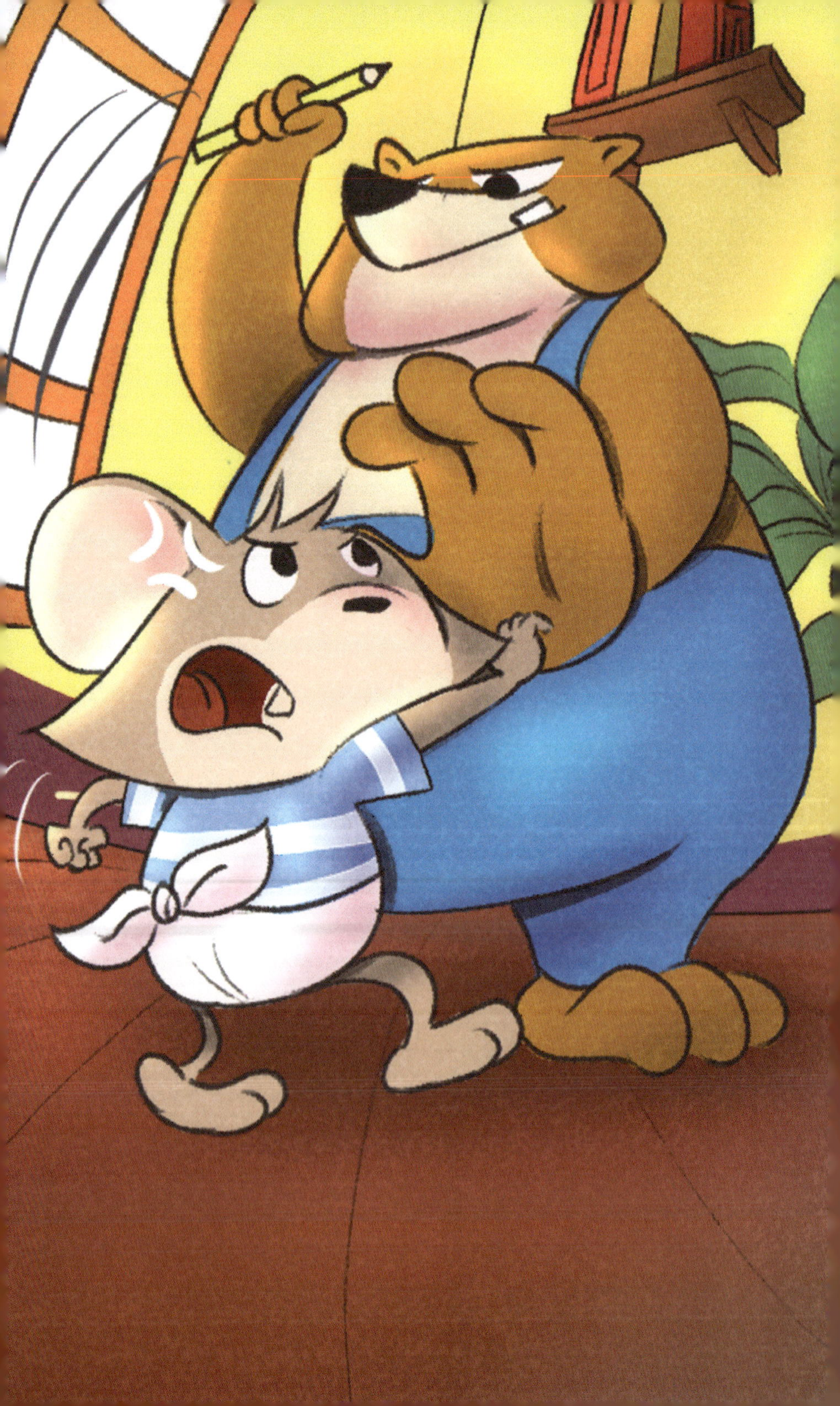

But in the afternoon, as Samy feared, Pip, the naughty boy, took his pencil again, but Samy was determined to be strong like brave Jack. He will ask him bravely to return his pencil.

" Can you give me back my pencil Pip, Its mine, and I need it now!" Can you help Samy say that bravely, but nicely?

HA HA HA HA

But Pip snapped,
"No! I won't give
it back!"
And he ran off with
Samy's pencil.
everyone turned
to look at them,

Samy's stomach butterflies were about to come, but he heard Mummy's voice, "Use your brain, you can be stronger!"

Samy thought hard and Ta Da, he had an idea! Can you help Samy think what to do? What will you do in this case?

Pip was bragging about his new sharpener all morning, he was sure Pip wouldn't like it if he took it!

"If you don't give me back my pencil, I will not give you your sharpener!" Samy said firmly and bravely.

Pip saw his new sharpener in Samy's hand and came running to snatch it.

But suddenly, he slipped on Lilly's splash of water from her water bottle.

Pip slid over the floor and crashed into the toy cabinet

SLIP SLIP

Can you try to show us how Pip fell ?
but be careful this is pretend play!

Everyone laughed! Samy walked up to Pip, he knew how it felt when you are laughed at!

He did not laugh, he helped Pip up, took his pencil and said,

"You shouldn't have taken what is not yours Pip!"

HA HA

He was very brave, "Please never take my things again!"

Suddenly there was a clap!

Teacher was standing and clapping, "Well done Samy, that was very brave and very kind!"

Everyone joined and clapped for Samy. he felt proud, just like brave Jack ,

"I shall always be strong, brave and kind in future," he said to himself.

Can you say that to yourself?
Yes always remember to be like
Brave Jack, Strong, Brave and Kind.

Printed in Great Britain
by Amazon